I0837642

Written : Isela Arredondo
Editor: Marlenee Padilla
Graphic Design and Illustration:
Juana Jasmin Barron Bautista

Library of Congress Control Number: 2023900022
ISBN: 9798986457383
www.theartistwithinfoundation.com

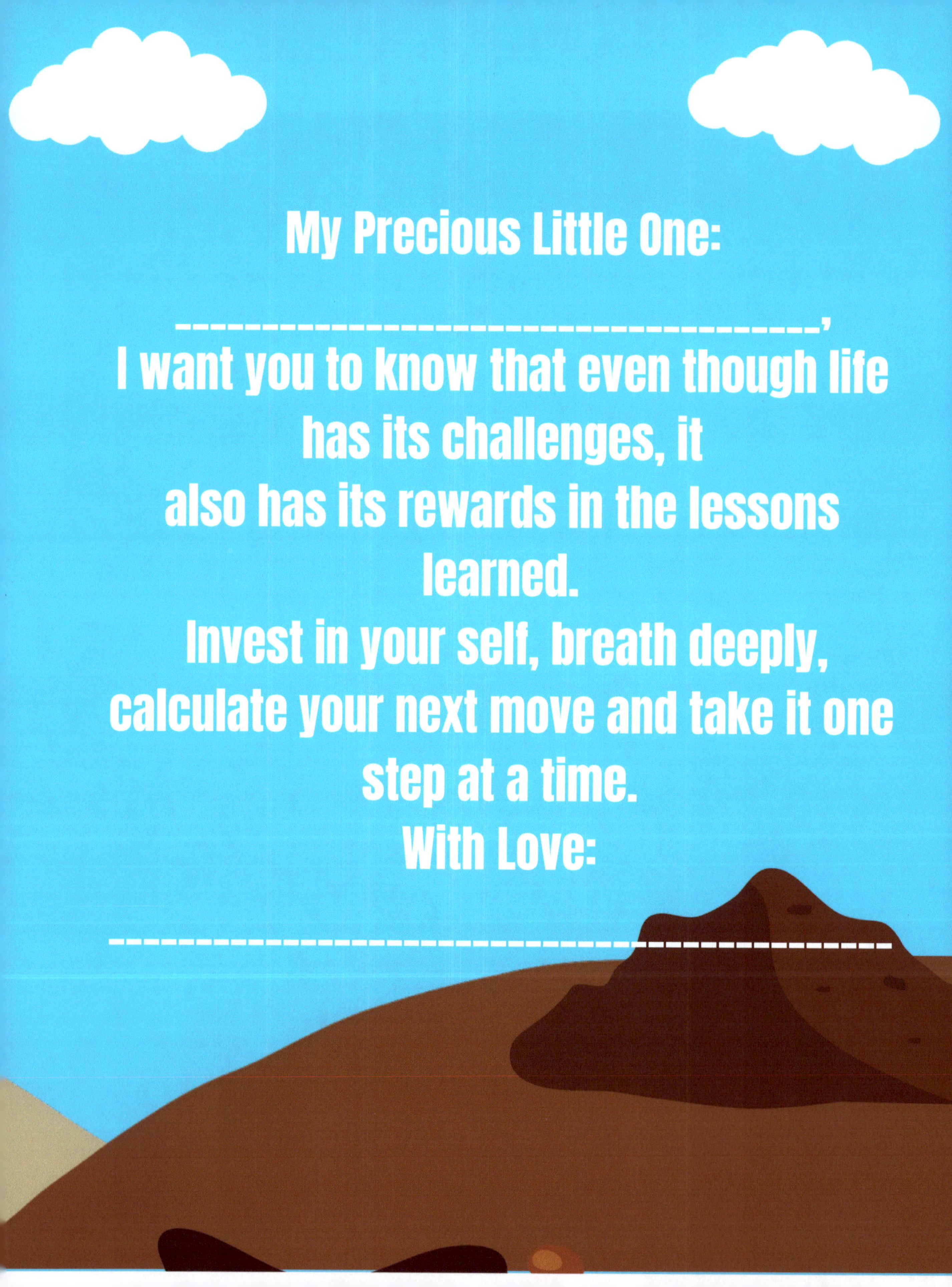

My Precious Little One:

____,
I want you to know that even though life
has its challenges, it
also has its rewards in the lessons
learned.
Invest in your self, breath deeply,
calculate your next move and take it one
step at a time.
With Love:

____

Why do you say that
life is like a tunnel?

My Little Wiggle Worm, both,
sometimes go up and sometimes go
down.

You must always focus on your next wiggle and tunnel towards your next adventure.

But what if it's as hard as climbing uphill?

You must wiggle, wiggle,
Wiggle Worm.

Challenge yourself and before you know it, you will be closer to your goal to conquer each hill.

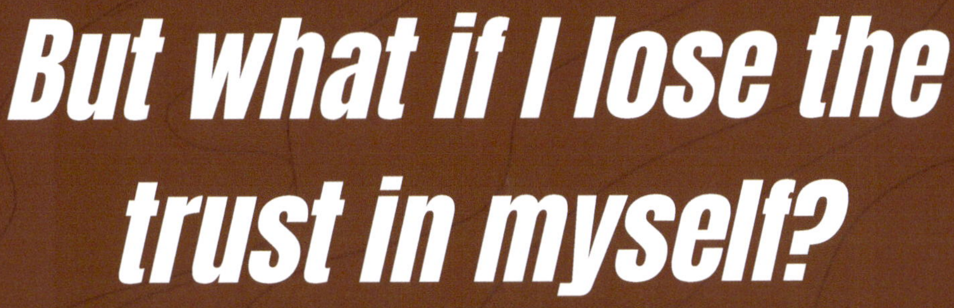

Trust is the result of well thought out actions,

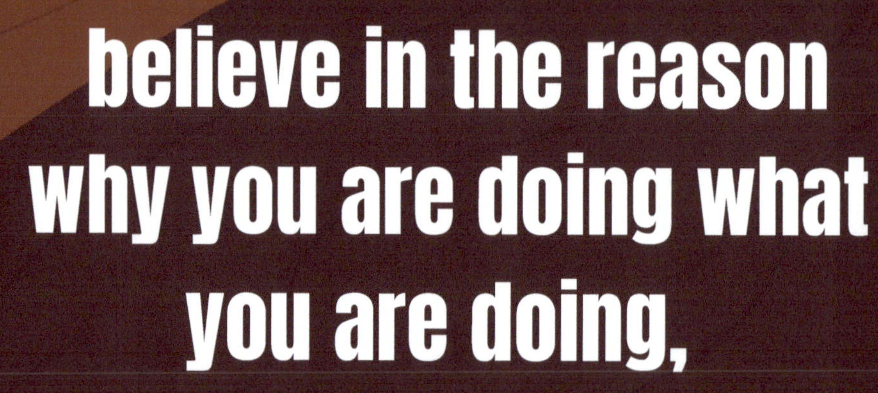
believe in the reason
why you are doing what
you are doing,

and before you
know it,

you will learn to trust yourself again.

But what if I feel alone?

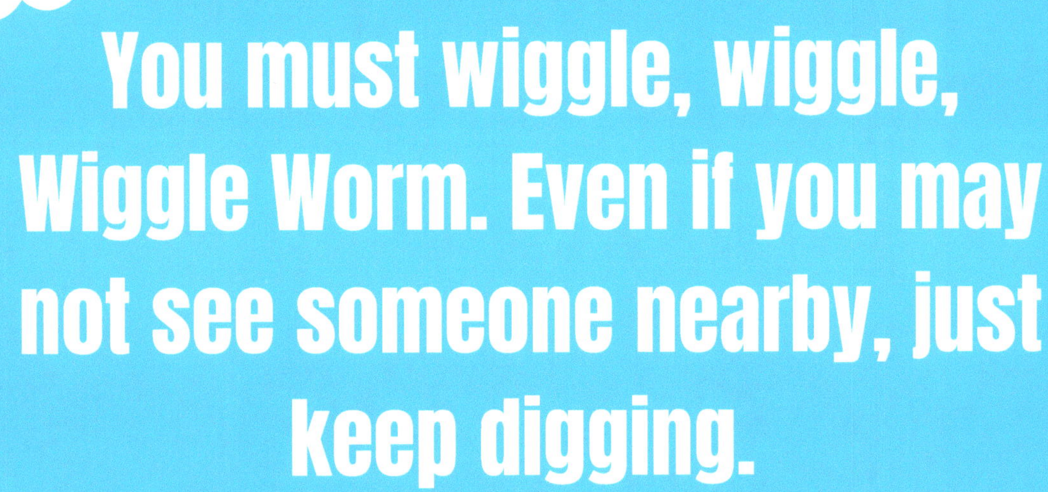
You must wiggle, wiggle,
Wiggle Worm. Even if you may
not see someone nearby, just
keep digging.

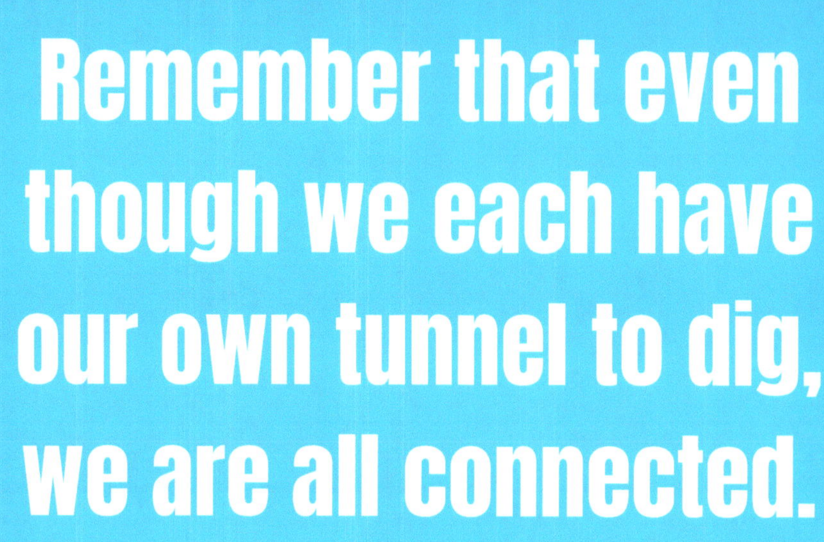

Remember that even
though we each have
our own tunnel to dig,
we are all connected.

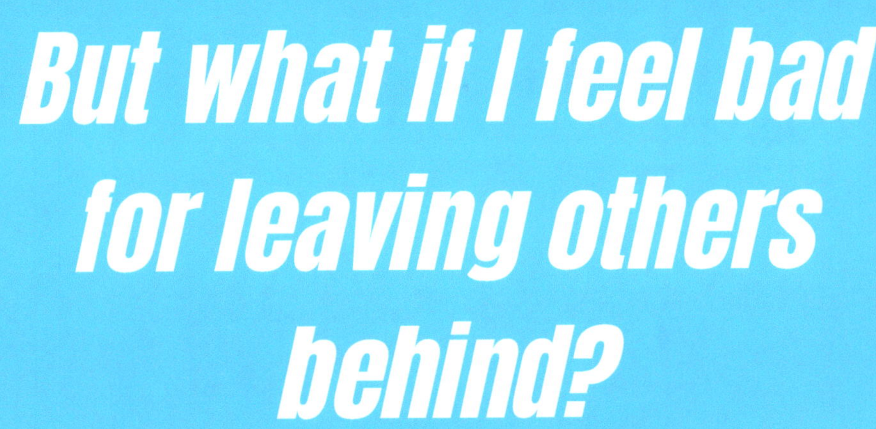

But what if I feel bad for leaving others behind?

You are not leaving anyone behind.

You're simply making another
tunnel that they can follow,

until they get the
strength to dig their
own and you
can meet again.

But what if my heart
feels as heavy as an
anchor?

An anchor and our heart, like a bucket,
can carry a lot of heavy things,

learn to leave or let go of
heavy things or feelings so you
can float.

But what if I wiggle so hard, only to end up in the wrong tunnel?

You must you wiggle wiggle, Wiggle Worm.

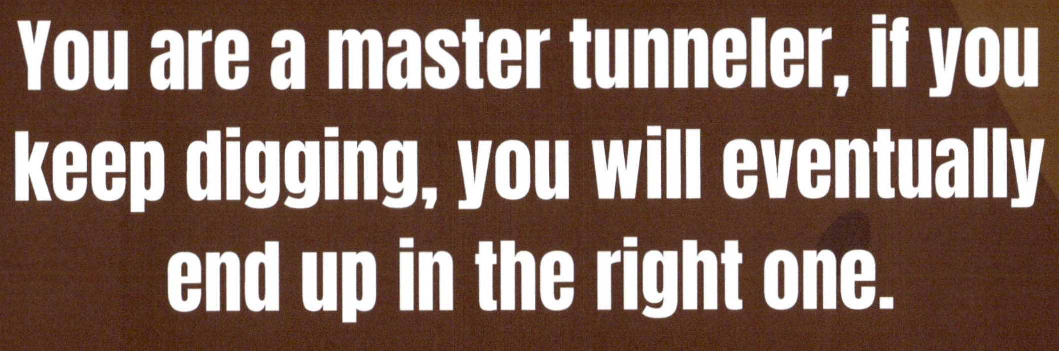

You are a master tunneler, if you keep digging, you will eventually end up in the right one.

But what if the rain pours down like a river and I feel like I'm drowning?

The rains will come and they wil go.

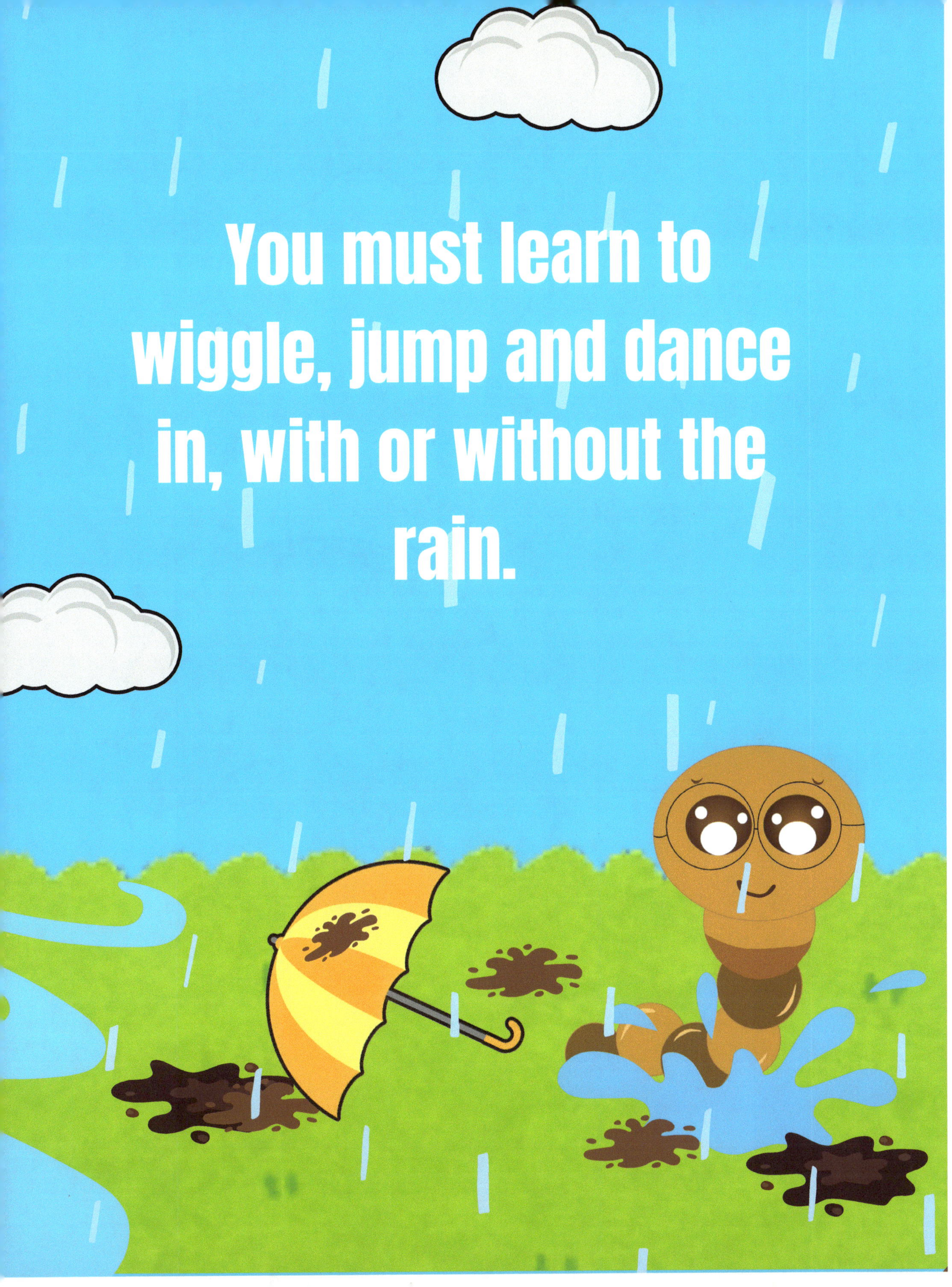
You must learn to wiggle, jump and dance in, with or without the rain.

But what if I am so tired and I just cannot wiggle one more wiggle?

You must wiggle wiggle, Wiggle Worm
to a place where you
can rest.

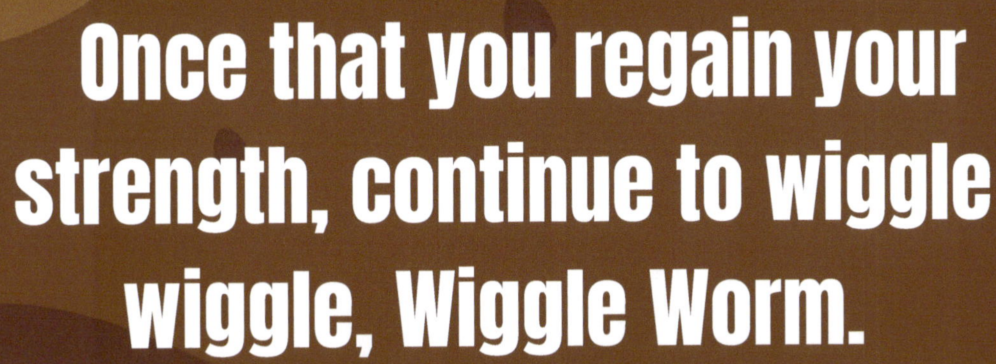

Once that you regain your strength, continue to wiggle wiggle, Wiggle Worm.

But what if I get hurt, cut, or bleed?

You must wiggle wiggle, Wiggle Worm. Sometimes you can't avoid getting hurt. Take care of your injury,

eventually it will heal and you will learn that what once hurt, does not hurt forever.

But what if I am blocked by a mountain like rock?

You must recognize that a rock is a rock regardless the size.

Focus on how you can go around, over or through the obstacle.

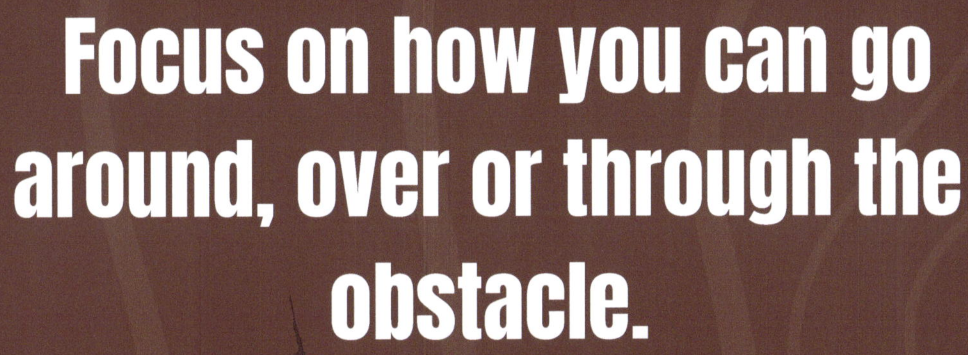

And remember that the only true obstacles
are those we choose to do nothing about.

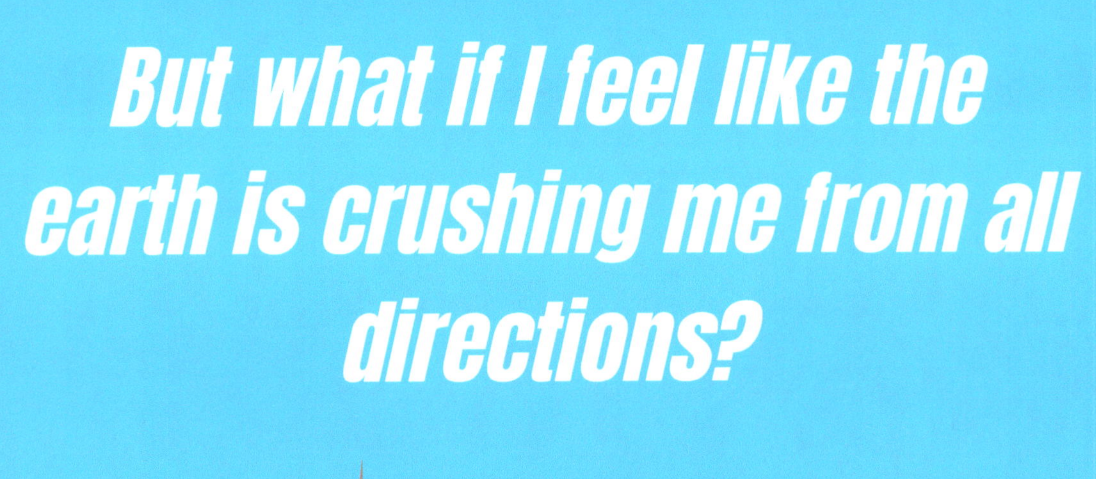

But what if I feel like the earth is crushing me from all directions?

You must wiggle, wiggle, Wiggle Worm.

Sometimes you will feel great pressure.

Remember to take a
deep breath, close
your eyes, quiet your
heart ....

and truly listen. What do you hear?
wiggle

wiggle
me too
I can wiggle

All our friends feel and press forward in the same way.

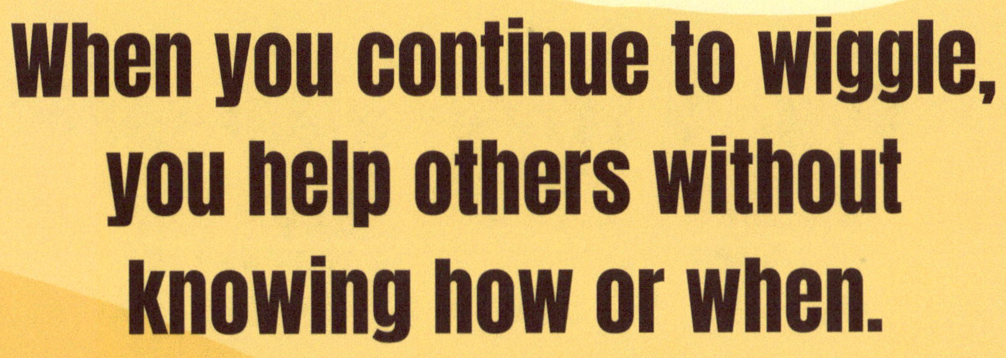

When you continue to wiggle,
you help others without
knowing how or when.

Be the hero and always wiggle, wiggle, Wiggle Worm.

Cool Fact:

- Worms have no eyes, ears, or lungs!
- Worms rely on their skin to breathe, and though they don't have eyes, they can sense light and vibrations. This could be tied to the idea that, even when the path isn't clear, we can still "feel" our way forward and trust our instincts.
- Worms make the soil healthy.
- Worms help create rich soil by breaking down organic matter and turning it into nutrient-rich castings. You can use this as a metaphor for how hard work (like digging through challenges) can turn into something positive and fruitful for ourselves and others.
- Worms are both male and female (hermaphrodites).
- Worms have both male and female reproductive organs, which makes them very unique! This could be subtly incorporated to promote the idea of self-sufficiency and that, just like worms, we have everything within ourselves to succeed.
- Worms can regenerate lost body parts.
- Some species of worms can regenerate parts of their body if they're cut or injured. This ties in perfectly with your themes of healing and resilience, showing kids that they can "bounce back" from tough times, just like a worm.
- Worms are important for the ecosystem.
- Worms play a vital role in the ecosystem by aerating the soil and helping plants grow. This can reflect the message of community and connectedness, showing that even though each worm (or person) is on their own journey, they contribute to the world in important ways.
- Worms move by wiggling their muscles.
- Worms move by contracting and expanding their muscles, creating that iconic "wiggle" motion. This can reinforce the message of steady, continuous effort–no matter how small the movement, progress is always being made!
- Worms can tunnel several feet underground.
- Some worms are known to dig tunnels up to six feet deep! You can use this to show how persistence pays off, and even when it seems like you've got a long way to go, steady wiggling will get you there.
- Worms prefer the dark.
- Worms avoid sunlight and spend their time underground in the dark, moist earth. This could be linked to the idea that, even when things seem dark or uncertain, a worm keeps moving forward, trusting the path ahead.